DOG IN CHARGE

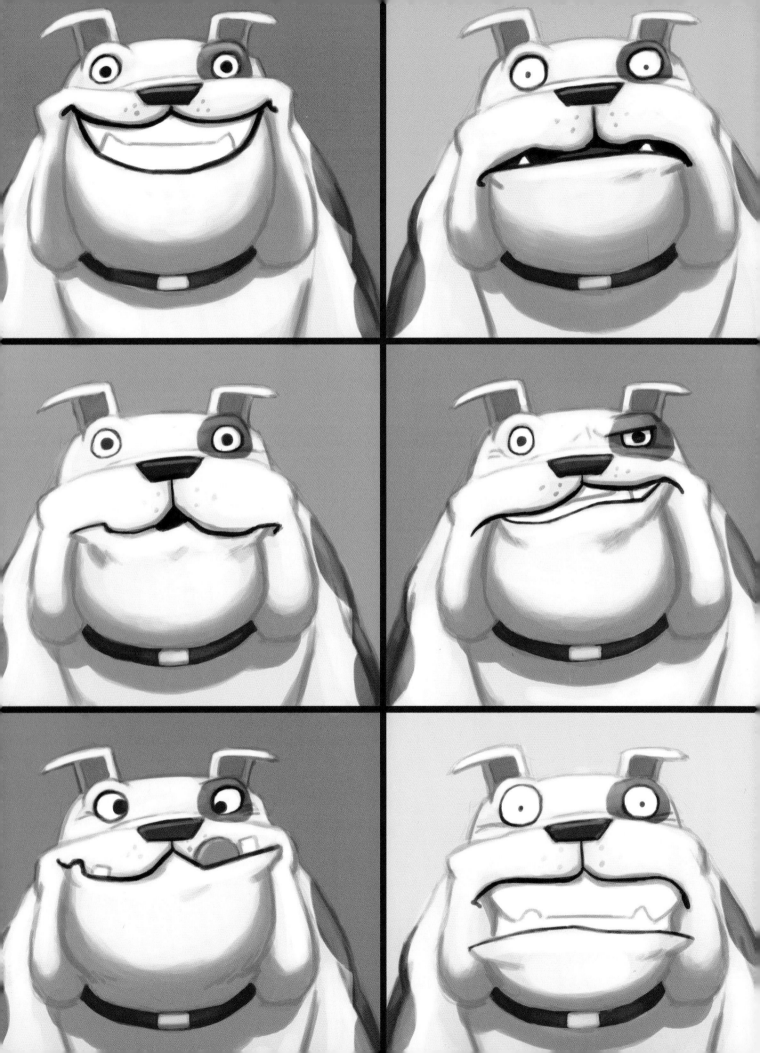

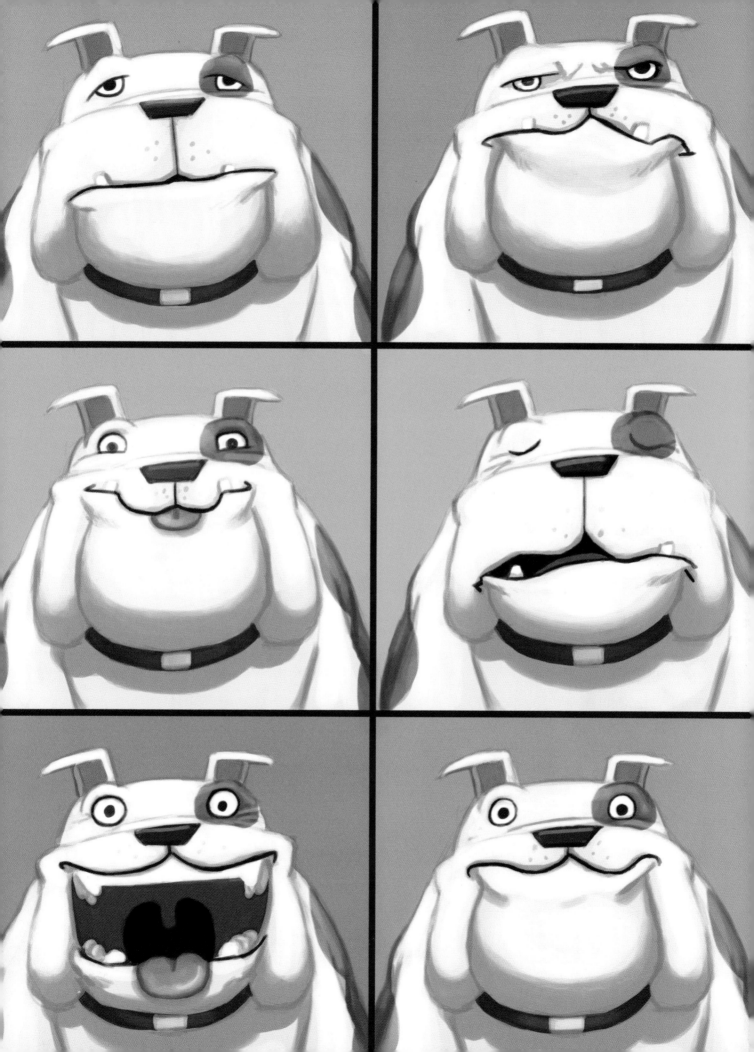

DOG IN CHARGE

by **K. L. GOING**   illustrated by **DAN SANTAT**

SCHOLASTIC INC.

For Roxanne, the very best dog, and for my dad, who loved her.
—K.L.G.

For Leah, Alek, and Kyle.
—D.S.

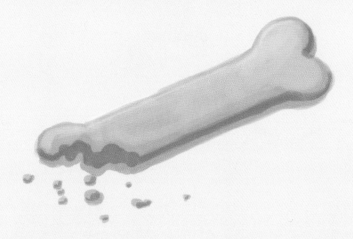

ISBN 978-0-545-50019-7

Text copyright © 2012 by K. L. Going.
Pictures copyright © 2012 by Dan Santat.
All rights reserved. Published by Scholastic Inc.,
557 Broadway, New York, NY 10012,
by arrangement with Dial Books for Young Readers,
a division of Penguin Young Readers Group,
a member of Penguin Group (USA) Inc.
SCHOLASTIC and associated logos are trademarks
and/or registered trademarks of Scholastic Inc.

12 11 10 9 8 7 6 5 4 3 2   12 13 14 15 16 17/0

Printed in the U.S.A.   08

First Scholastic printing, September 2012

Designed by Jasmin Rubero
Text set in Archer with Sassoon Infant Com

Dog had a busy afternoon.

Then Dog got a scrumptious dog treat.

"Oh boy, oh boy, oh boy!"

thought Dog.

"Good Dog. Smart Dog. The very best Dog. We're going to the store, so now you will be in charge. Watch the cats, and make sure they don't get in any mischief."

The family bustled and hustled out the door,
into the car.

Dog watched them go,
eyeing the cats lined up in a row.

"First we will sit and then we will stay," thought Dog.

But the cats did not sit.
Where did all the cats go?
There were one, two, three, four, five empty spots.

Dog chased the cat into the living room.

No cat.

Or was there?

"Out," barked Dog.

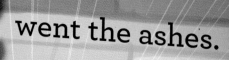
went the ashes.

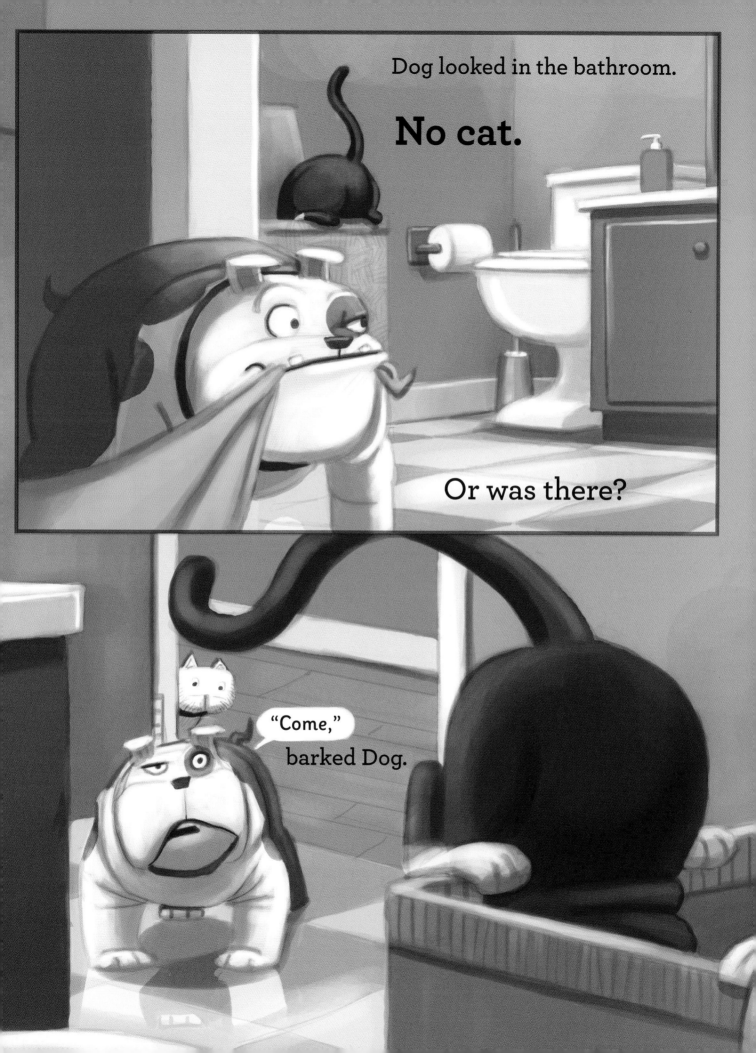

KERPLOOIE! went the clothes in the hamper.

Where were all the cats?

Soon the family would come home.
Would he still be a good Dog, a smart Dog, the very best Dog?
Would he get more scrumptious dog treats?

It was hard to be in charge.
Dog was hungry and tired.
He lay down to think.

Then Dog
had an idea.

Dog headed for
the kitchen.

Treats for
good cats!

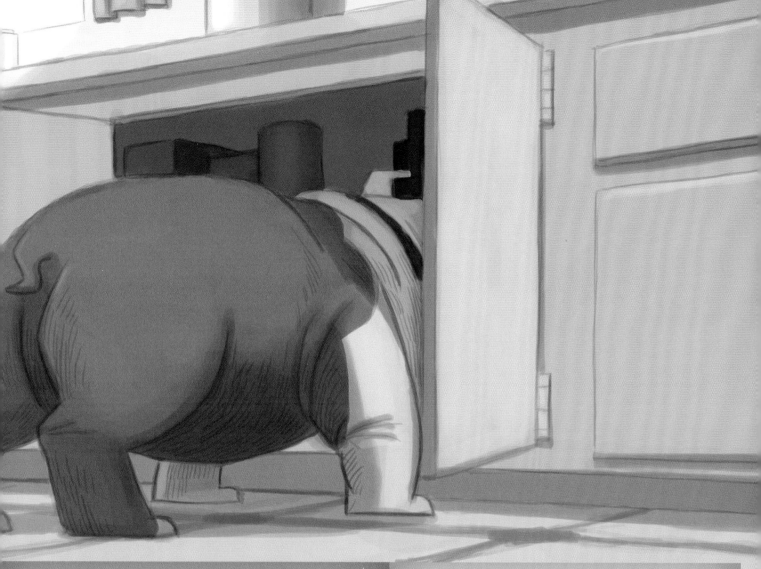

Dog's tummy rumbled.

Dog's nose twitched.

Dog's mouth opened.

Dog ate one, two, **three, four, five** cat treats.

Soon the bag
was empty.

Poor Dog!

The family would not let him be
in charge again.

Dog had to fix everything.
He tried to think, but his eyes
grew heavy and his paw was soft.

Then one, two, **three**, **four**, **five** little noses appeared.

PURR

went the cats.
They loved Dog.

GOOD KITTY
CAT TREATS

So one, two, three, four, five cats licked up the crumbs and milk.

One, two, three, four, five cats polished the living room.

One, two, **three**, **four**, **five** cats
neatened the bedroom.

One, two, **three**, **four**, **five** cats
straightened the bathroom.

Then one, two, three, four, five cats snuggled up next to Dog.

The sound of a car
rumbled in the driveway.

The
family
was home.

Dog got lots of scrumptious dog treats.

"Were the cats good while you were in charge?"

Dog barked.

He stood on his back legs and danced in a circle.

"Good cats,"

thought Dog.

"Smart cats.
The very best cats."

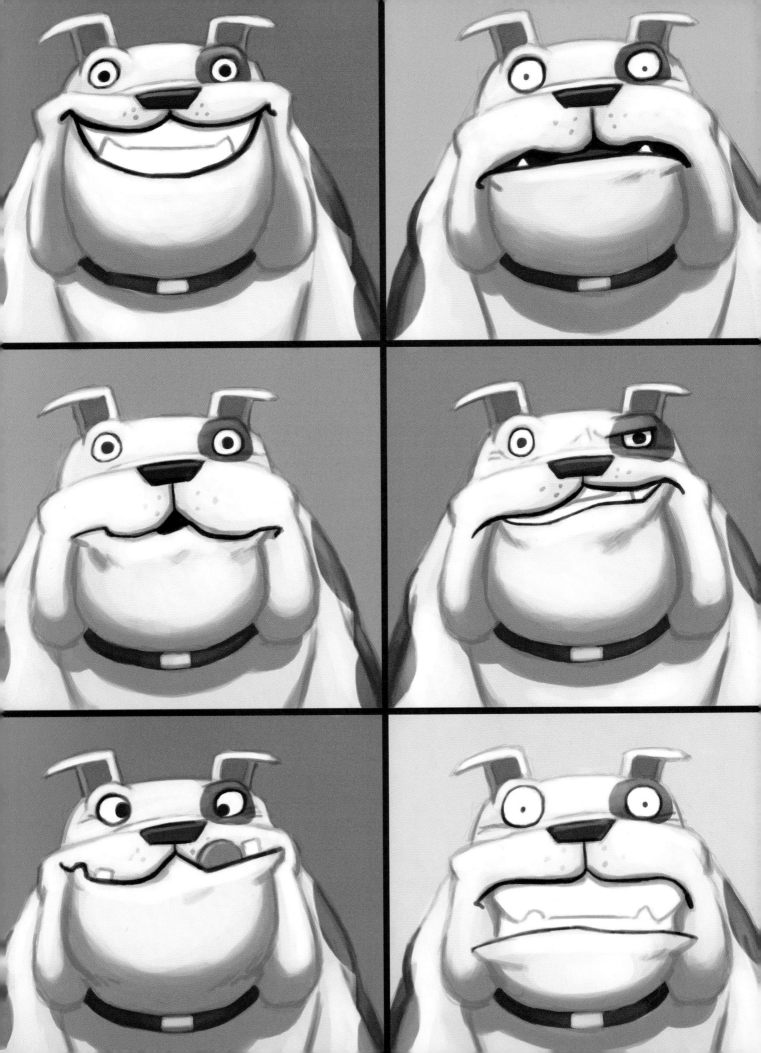

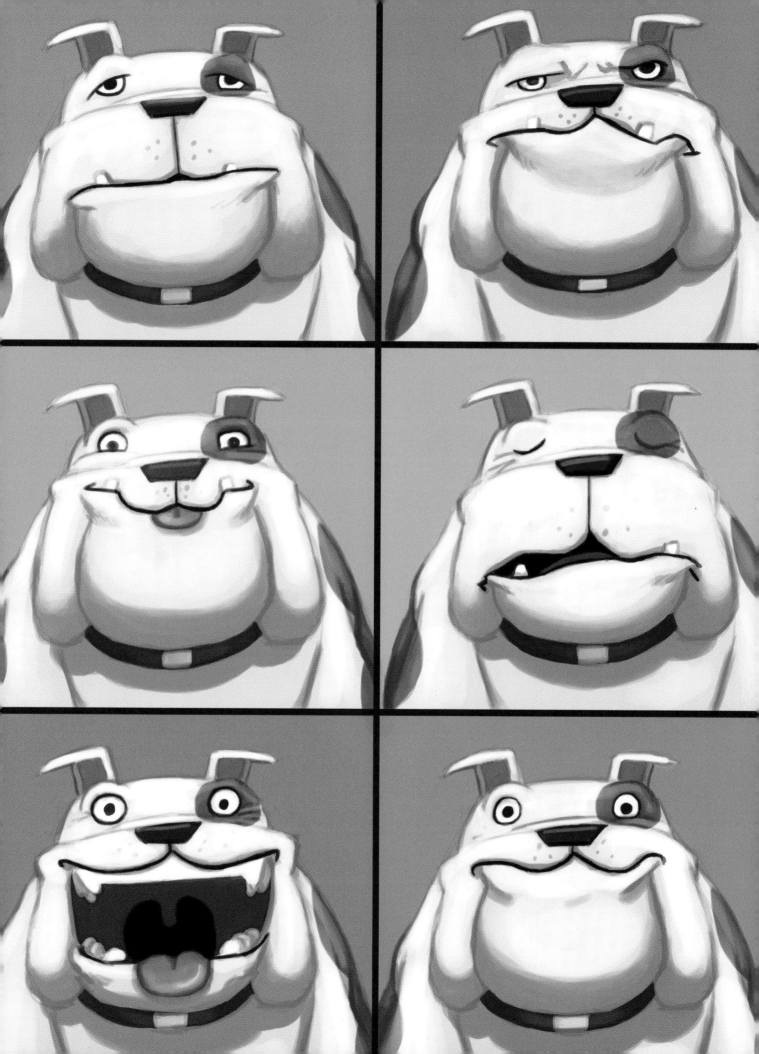